And so Eppie  eg in the crocodile's ile continued laughi and louder he la ey echoed with his guffaws and fairytale creatures came from all over the kingdom to the edge of the pond to see what was happening.

'Oh no!' cried Rapunzel, who'd jumped out of her tower to come and see what all the kerfuffle was about. 'I suspect that's the same crocodile that ate Captain Hook's hand. In fact, I suspect that little girl is going to get her leg bitten off if we don't do something about it.'

Also available by
Gretel Killeen in Red Fox

my Sister's a Full Stop

MY SISTER'S A FULL STOP
A RED FOX BOOK 0 099 46408 X

Published in Great Britain by Red Fox,
an imprint of Random House Children's Books

First published in Australia by Random House Australia Pty Ltd 2000
Red Fox edition published 2004

1 3 5 7 9 10 8 6 4 2

Papers used by Random House Children's Books are natural, recyclable products
made from wood grown in sustainable forests. The manufacturing processes conform
to the environmental regulations of the country of origin.

Red Fox books are published by Random House Children's Books,
61–63 Uxbridge Road, London W5 5SA,
a division of The Random House Group Ltd,
in Australia by Random House Australia (Pty) Ltd,
20 Alfred Street, Milsons Point, Sydney, NSW 2061, Australia,
in New Zealand by Random House New Zealand Ltd,
18 Poland Road, Glenfield, Auckland 10, New Zealand,
and in South Africa by Random House (Pty) Ltd,
Endulini, 5A Jubilee Road, Parktown 2193, South Africa

THE RANDOM HOUSE GROUP Limited Reg. No. 954009

www.kidsatrandomhouse.co.uk

A CIP catalogue record for this book is available from the British Library.

Printed and bound in Great Britain by Cox & Wyman Ltd, Reading, Berkshire

gretEl KiLLeen

my Sister's a Full Stop

Illustrated by
Zeke and **Eppie**

RED FOX

A message from your author...

G'day from the land down under where our world is very similar to yours but the animals are **weirder**, the sun is **hotter** and the space much much **bigger**. As you know we speak the same language as you so even if you have **squirrels in your hair** and a **wombat up your nose** you'll be able to understand this story. Although, it did occur to me while I was riding my kangaroo up to the shops this morning that maybe there is one word in this book that you might not have come across before and that word is **bindi-eye**. A bindi-eye is a type of prickle that grows on a plant that grows in the grass, and it **really hurts** if you tread on one. Why only the other day I trod on a bindi-eye myself but luckily an emu was passing by at the time and she gave me a **witchety grub lolly** to take my mind off the pain. So I'm all better and now all I hope is that you love this fifth book in the *My Sister's* series.

So **cheers Big Ears** and I look forward to meeting you one day in the magical land of **Oz-tralia!**

It's not every day that you get stuck inside the story of a book. But then it's not every day that your sister shrinks to the size of a strawberry, gets a yo-yo tangled in her hair and ends up in outer space where she has to be rescued by you! And it's not every day that you return from space riding on a meteor and the amazing speed stretches you and your sister very long and thin like pieces of spaghetti so that when you finally do get home you get sucked down the bathroom

plughole. Oh no, it's not every day that
you end up in the pipes and drains under
your house, get zapped by an electric eel,
snuggled by a shark (who's pretending to
be seaweed), rescued by a merprincess,
attacked by soldier crabs, and disguised as
sea slugs. And it's not every day that you
get stranded on a desert island, evaporated
like water droplets, and delivered by the
stork to your very own back garden
where your mother promptly swallows
you and your sister! So, it's not every day
that you have to travel all the way
through your mother's veins and gizzards
and heart and brain to save your mum's
life and then finally escape out of her
nose by getting splattered in a sneeze with
huge blobs of snot . . . and squished right
inside the book of fairytales she's
reading. But that's what had happened so
far today.

'Mmmmm yum,' slurped the Big Bad Wolf as he licked his big bad lips. 'So, what have we here?'

'Should we answer?' whispered Eppie as she lay with Zeke on the Emerald Forest floor in precisely the spot where they'd snot-landed.

'Why would we do that, Eppie?' said Zeke. 'Did your mind fly out of your ear when we were blown out of Mum's nose, or has your brain just passed its use-by date and it's time to buy you a fresh one?'

'Well at least I *have* a brain,' said Eppie. 'Unlike you, who just has a sadly empty head with a peanut rolling round inside it.'

'Do not,' said Zeke.

'Do so,' said Eppie.

'Do not,' said Zeke.

'Do so,' said Eppie.

'Do not,' said Zeke.

'Do so,' said Eppie.

'Do not,' said Zeke.

'Do so,' said Eppie.

'Do not,' said Zeke.

'Do so,' said Eppie.

'Do not,' said Zeke.

'Do so,' said Eppie.

'Do not,' said Zeke.

'Do so,' said Eppie.

'Aslurp ahum,'

slobbered the Big Bad Wolf. 'Excuse me for interrupting your argument, but I said, *What have we here?*'

'You tell him,' whispered Eppie.

'No, you tell him,' said Zeke.

'No, you,' said Eppie.

'No, you, you prawnbottom,' said Zeke.

Eppie poked her tongue out at Zeke and said, 'Eeeee ould ah ar eai i oo o u a ar!'

'Would you mind repeating that with your big fat tongue back inside your mouth!' whispered Zeke, just before he poked his own tongue out so incredibly far that he looked like a spineless spiny anteater.

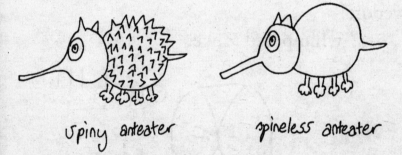

spiny anteater   spineless anteater

So Eppie put her tongue back inside her mouth and whispered, 'I said, we should answer the wolf because it's very rude not to answer when someone asks you a question.'

'Oh really, Miss Goody-Two-Shoes Fart-a-Lot Teacher's Pet,' said Zeke. 'Well, why don't you answer the question and while the wolf is eating you I'll run away and be free and live happily ever after.'

'Well, you won't be living happily ever after if you run away,' replied Eppie, 'because after I've been eaten I'm going to come back and haunt you and every second of every day I'm going to sneak up behind you, grab the top of your undies and give you an enormous wedgie!'

'Ouch,' whimpered Zeke.

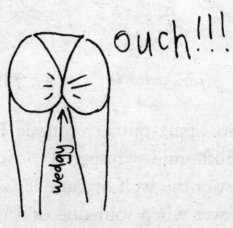

'Mmmmmmmmmmmmmmmmmmmmmm,' murmured the Big Bad Wolf while his big bad stomach rumbled like a big bad ball of thunder. 'I'm getting impatient, so you'd better tell me: # What have we here?'

'Go on, Miss Goody-Goody, I dare you,' said Zeke. 'I dare you to tell him your name and your age and your weight and your height and that you personally recommend he eat you with a touch of tomato sauce and perhaps a piece of garlic bread and a glass of orange squash.'

'Did someone say squash?' giggled the Big Bad Wolf. 'I love to drink a glass of squash when I eat and I like to eat absolutely everything and anything in the whole wide world . . . except potatoes, of course.'

7

'Quick!' Eppie whispered to Zeke. 'Quick, pretend you're a potato!'

'What!!!!!!!!!!!!'

said Zeke.

'I said, pretend you're a potato,' whispered Eppie.

'There's no need to speak in that smarty-pants voice,' sniffed Zeke. 'It makes you sound exactly like my teacher Miss Snailheadface, and she knows as much about anything as a dead bug stuck in ear wax.'

'All right, Zeke,' responded Eppie. 'Have it your way. I'll curl up like a potato and you jump up and down like a boy's bra-bum-face with a dillion ants in his pants and we'll see which one of us the Big Bad Wolf eats . . . But then, on the other hand, Zeke, you may not need to do a thing because you actually already look so disgusting that only a blind boa constrictor who'd been hit on the head by a bucket full of spit would ever want to eat you.'

'You're just jealous,' Zeke replied, 'because I'm such a chick magnet.' Then he curled up on the ground and tried to look like a potato.

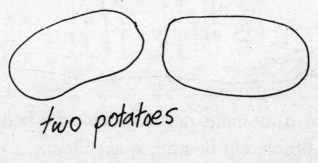

two potatoes

'Well, that doesn't make sense,' said the Big Bad Wolf as he sniffed the air and looked at Zeke and Eppie. 'My nose smells humans but my eyes see potatoes! What's wrong with me? I think I'd better lie down.'

And with that the Big Bad Wolf lay on the ground, with his legs poking straight up into the air. 'Quick, someone get me a doctor,' he roared. And then his eyes rolled round like two brown ferris wheels and some pukey saliva dribbled out of his mouth. 'Oh Mummy,' he sighed, 'I'm feeling d-i-z-z-y.' And then he promptly fainted.

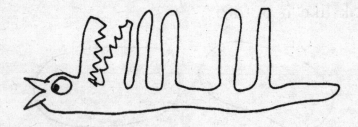

For a moment nothing could be heard but absolutely deathly quiet silence.

Shshshshshshshshshshshshshshshshshshshshs hshshshshshshshshshshshshshshshshshsh.

And then all of a sudden the forest was filled with the thunderous sound of hooves, paws and wings as all the animals of the Emerald Forest leapt from their trees and climbed from their burrows and came galumping, crawling, flying and slithering straight towards Eppie and Zeke.

'Heeeeeeeeee eeeeelp!' squealed Eppie and Zeke as they picked themselves up from the ground and began to run as fast as they could every which way to escape from the thousands of creatures.

'Run!' yelled Zeke.

'Ah der,' yelled Eppie.

'Follow me,' said Zeke.

'No, follow me,' said Eppie.

'No, follow me,' said Zeke.

'No, follow me,' said Eppie.

'No, follow me,' said Zeke.
'No, follow me,' said Eppie.
'No, follow me,' said Zeke.
'No, follow me,' said Eppie.
And so Eppie and Zeke ran around in a circle, with each one thinking the other one was following them. Around . . . and around . . . and around they went, while the thousands of forest creatures got closer

Aaagh

and closer

and closer.

'Stop them!' trumpeted a voice from above.

'Stop them,' repeated the voice as the sun was hidden behind a huge shape that looked like a balloon with two wings and a hose, sitting on top of a magic carpet.

'Stooooooooop them!' screeched the voice, sounding very like a trombone that couldn't reach the highest note. Then a slow, steady flapping came closer and closer and with a thump King Bumbo crash-landed.

'Stop them,' King Bumbo repeated weakly as he vacuumed the dust off himself with his trunk.

But no one could stop them, until the forest began to rattle with a steady **thump**, thump. It was the sound of something enormous climbing down a very, very tall beanstalk.

The ground shook, the land was in shadow and with a rustle and a sigh an enormous hand scooped down low and collected the trembling Zeke and Eppie in the cup of its huge sausage fingers.

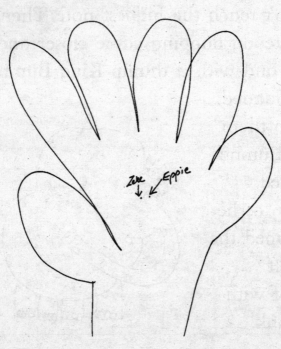

Zeke ↓   ↙ Eppie

'Thank you, giant,' roared King Bumbo as he bumbled up to the huge giant's feet. 'Thank you so much from the bottom of my heart for gently capturing our heroes.'

'I beg your pardon,' yelled the gigantic giant from his very great height – taller than the tallest building that you've ever seen.

'What?' called King Bumbo.

'Pardon,' bellowed the giant.

'What?' said King Bumbo, holding his big left foot up to his ear.

'What?' said the giant.

'Pardon?' said King Bumbo.

'What?'

'Pardon?'

'What?'

'Pardon?'

'What?'

'Pardon?'

'What?'

'Oh for heaven's sake' interrupted
Tunkerbell as she flew towards King
Bumbo and landed
right between his
eyes. 'You tell me
what you want to
tell the giant, and I'll
tinker up and tell him.'

'Oh, thank you, Tunkerbell,' sighed King
Bumbo as he crossed his eyes to look at
her. 'Just tell him to lean forward please so
that our mouths and ears are closer.'

'Okey-tinkdokey,' tinkled Tunkerbell. 'I'll
be back in about half an hour.' And off
she flew with a wisp of magic dust and
the gentle tinkling of the bells on her
shoes.

'Half an hour!' moaned the white
rabbit. 'I can't wait that long . . . I'm late,
I'm late, for a very important date!'

16

'Half an hour,' said Rumpelstiltskin. 'That's absolutely ridiculous! Can somebody wake me when it's all sorted out because I'm going to have a quick snooze.'

A slow snooze   A quick snooze

'**Half an hour,**' groaned Zeke and Eppie from high up in the giant's hand.

'How boring,' moaned Zeke. 'What will we do? There isn't even a TV to watch here.'

'We could play I-spy, while we wait,' said Eppie.

'Why do you always say you want to play I-spy?' sighed Zeke. 'Have you lost something? Do you need glasses? Or are you just a boring old toad?'

'Crebbit,' said Eppie, puffing out her cheeks and trying to look like a toad.

'Double crebbit,' said Zeke.

And so Zeke and Eppie passed the half hour in the creative way that they always passed the time away . . . by arguing with each other.

'Well if I'm a toad, you must be a toad too,' said Eppie, 'and Mum must be a toad as well.'

'Not necessarily,' said Zeke as he tried to make himself burp. 'You might have been swapped in the hospital when my real sister was born.'

'Maybe you were the one who was swapped,' said Eppie. 'And one day your real family will come and get you and take you back to the land of bums.'

'Oh ha ha,' said Zeke.

'Yes, ha ha, ha ha,' said Eppie.

'Well, ha ha ha ha ha ha ha ha ha ha ha ha ha,' said Zeke.

'Well, ha ha ha ha ha ha ha ha ha ha ha ha ha ha ha ha ha ha ha ha ha ha ha ha ha ha ha ha ha ha ha ha ha ha ha ha ha ha ha ha ha ha ha ha ha ha ha ha ha ha ha ha ha ha ha ha.'

'Be quiet, tiny people,' yelled the giant, 'I'm trying to listen to Tunkerbell.'

blah blah
Giant blah
blah

And so Tunkerbell whispered in the giant's ear and asked him to please lean his ears and mouth closer down to Bumbo's.

'Oh yuck, why?' said the giant, quite outraged. 'Does he want to kiss and hug me!'

'No,' said Tunkerbell, patting the giant on his back with her shiny, tiny right wing. 'He wants to tell you something.'

'Well I'm afraid you'll have to tell Bumbo that I can't possibly bend down that far,' said the giant, 'and Bumbo is simply going to have to come up here.'

'Okey-tinkdokey,' tinkled Tunkerbell, and then she flew back down to Bumbo.

'**What!!!!!!!!**' roared King Bumbo when Tunkerbell had finished speaking. 'How on earth am I supposed to get up that high? I'm an elephant, not a fire cracker! My maximum height is fifteen storeys and the giant's head is so far up it even pokes through the clouds.'

'Ah, excuse me,' said a voice a little like Sylvester Stallone's.

'Yes,' said King Bumbo, 'and who are you?'

'Well, sir, I'm the flying unicorn, and my name is Sylvester Stallion. So if you like you could sit on my back and I could fly you up to your meeting.'

'But how on earth can you fly that high?' asked King Bumbo.

'I'll start by bouncing off a trampoline,' said Sylvester Stallion-Unicorn.

'What trampoline?' said King Bumbo, sounding very irritated.

'Why, Papa Bear's tummy of course!' said Sylvester.

'Well, how much will the flight cost?' asked King Bumbo.

'That depends on whether you want a business or economy class ticket,' said Sylvester Stallion-Unicorn. 'With business class you get a hot meal during the flight and with economy class you only get a plastic container of orange juice, which quite frankly is almost impossible to open without spilling it all over yourself.'

'All right, I'll go business class,' said King Bumbo. 'Now hurry up and let's go.'

And so the seven dwarves lifted Bumbo onto the unicorn's back, and before a hot meal could even be organized, they had bounced off Papa Bear's tummy and were high up in the sky circling round the giant's head looking for somewhere safe to land.

All was going quite well as they flapped and buzzed around the giant's moppy hairdo until a set of clouds rolled up . . . and suddenly the unicorn couldn't see a thing.

'I can't see, I can't see,' squealed Sylvester Stallion-Unicorn. 'Mayday, mayday! I can't see a thing and I don't know which way is up or down!'

'Heeeeeeeeeeeeeeeeeeeeeeeeeeeeeeeeeeeeeeeeeeeeeeeeeeeeeeeeeeeeeeeeeeeeeeeeeeeeeeeeeeeeeeeeeeeeeeeeeeeeeeeeeeeeeelp!' roared King Bumbo.

‘Heeeeeeeeee
eeeeeeeeeeeee
eeeeeeeeeeeee
eeeeeeeeeeeeee
eeeeeeeeeeeee
eeeeeeeeeeeee
eeeeeeeeeeeee
eeeelp!’ spluttered Sylvester Stallion-Unicorn as he plummeted from the sky, pointy bit first, and landed right in the giant’s big toe . . . with King Bumbo still on his back.

‘Ouch, what was that?’ said the giant as he gently bent down and used his left hand to pluck the unicorn and the unicorn’s horn out of his big fat toe.

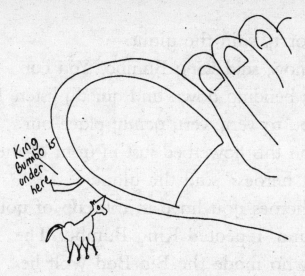

King Bumbo is under here

'Am I seeing things?' said Bumbo to the giant's head as it zooshed by his enormous ears. 'Am I seeing things, Giant, or are your mouth and ears suddenly right near mine?'

'Um,' mumbled the giant, stopping quite still.

'**Busted,** you lazy, selfish giant,' said King Bumbo. 'It appears you can bend down after all, and therefore could have saved us all a lot of time and bother if you'd only done so in the first place.'

'I'm sorry,' said the giant.

'Well now,' said King Bumbo. 'You can just stay bending down and quietly listen. I want you to very, very gently place our heroes on this flowerbed just in front of me.'

'What heroes?' said the giant.

'The heroes you have in the cup of your right hand,' repeated King Bumbo. 'The heroes who made the Big Bad Wolf lie down and fall unconscious so we can finally be rid of him and lock him up for good! So, if you give the heroes to me then, in exchange, I will give you seven hundred bananas.'

'Bananas?' said the giant in such a shocked voice that it sounded like finger-nails scraping down a blackboard. 'What do you think I could possibly do with seven hundred bananas?'

'All right, I'll give you seven hundred and fifty bananas,' responded King Bumbo.

'I don't think you get my point,' said the giant.

'All right,' said King Bumbo, 'I will now make my final offer. In exchange for the humans you have in your hand I will give you one thousand and five bananas.'

'Ooooooooooooooooooooooooooooooooo ooooooooooooooogh,' groaned the giant. 'I don't want any bananas at all.'

'Oh,' said King Bumbo. 'So you'll give me the heroes in return for nothing?'

'Hardly,' said the giant. 'I will exchange them for something I've wanted for ages.'

'What's that?' said King Bumbo.

'A live concert in my back yard, with a performance by Elton John, especially for my birthday next week.'

'Oh, no worries,' lied King Bumbo. 'I'll give him a call and send him right over.'

'Let's shake on it,' said the giant pleasantly.

'OK,' said King Bumbo, holding out his front foot.

'Good,' said the giant, reaching out his right hand.

'**Noooooooooooo ooooooooooooooo oooooooooooooooo ooooooooooooooo oooooooo!**'

roared all the creatures of the forest (including the hare and the tortoise, who had only just arrived).

'Don't open your hand!'

But it was already too late. And the creatures covered their eyes and held their breath as the giant opened his hand to shake King Bumbo's foot and Eppie and Zeke fell out of his hand and tumbled

down,

down,

down.

Well, Eppie landed plonk in a tree and stuck between two branches. But where was Zeke?

'Where is the other hero?' roared King Bumbo.

'I don't know,' said the giant. 'He must have fallen out and landed some other place.'

'That's not good enough,' bellowed King

HELP!

Bumbo. 'If you don't get him back to us within the hour then you will find that Elton John will certainly not be singing at your birthday party and I'll make sure all your friends give you really bad presents . . . like girls' underpants and small cans of beetroot.'

'Oh sob, sob, sob, sob,' blubbered the giant as his huge tears fell to the ground in enormous tidal waves. 'Please don't do that to me.'

'You have one hour to find the boy hero,' repeated King Bumbo grandly.

'Well then, I can promise you that if I do find the other hero I will eat him up for my birthday lunch, throw all my bad presents down on you from my castle and just play an Elton John CD.'

'Gasp!' gasped the creatures of the forest.

'Gasp!' gasped the Lion Queen.

30

'Gasp!' gasped Eppie, as she sat in a tree waiting to be rescued.

And 'Gasp!' gasped Zeke, just before he yelled,

'Come and get me, Eppie. I'm inside the giant's back pocket.'

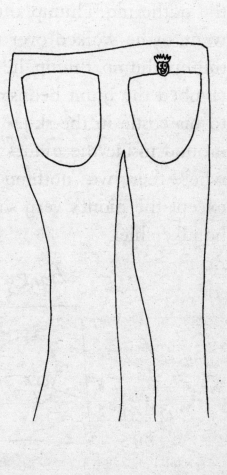

Luckily the giant didn't hear Zeke because he had stuck a finger in each ear so he could ignore King Bumbo. So, for a brief moment Zeke was sort of safe . . . until the giant turned in a huff and left the gathering. Thump, thump, thump, he went, as he walked over the forest and thump, thump, thump, he went, as he climbed the giant beanstalk to get back to his castle in the sky. And Zeke rumbled around inside the giant's back pocket, where there was nothing to play with except the giant's very snotty grubby old handkerchief.

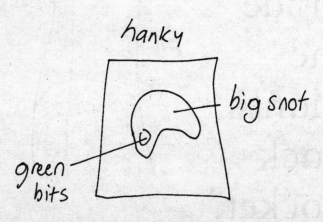

After a while Zeke began to get scared. But then just at that moment the giant let off a gigantic fart and Zeke took one accidental whiff . . . and then passed out.

Meanwhile, back in the forest, Eppie was slowly lowered from the tree, dangling from a chimpanzee's tail.

'Is she dead?' asked Snow White. 'Because if she is I have a lovely glass coffin she could lie in.'

'Wait,' said Prince Charming. 'Before you pronounce her dead, let me kiss her and see if she wakes.'

'What!' said Snow White. 'You want to kiss her! I thought that you loved *me*.'

'I do love you, Snow,' said Prince Charming, 'but you must understand it is my fairytale duty to kiss maidens in distress.'

'You must be joking,' said Snow White. 'There is no way I'm going to be your wife while you're still busy running around kissing every girl who has a bit of a problem.'

'Bit of a problem?' hissed Prince Charming. 'The little human just fell from the sky and landed in a tree. She is a poor unfortunate victim!'

'Can't you get Robin Hat to help her? He loves doing things for poor people.' Then Snow White called out through the forest in her shrill little voice, 'Robin Hat, Robin Hat, come and help us please.' And with the neigh of a horse but no horse in sight Robin Hat came galloping through the forest, dressed in a frock.

'I'm sorry it took me so long to get here,' said Robin Hat, 'but it's very difficult to run in high heels.'

'Of course,' said Prince Charming, charmingly.

'But why are you wearing high heels?' asked Snow White. 'And come to think of it, why are you dressed like a woman?'

'Because,' fumed Robin Hat, 'the Merry Men stole my clothes and this frock is all I could find. I took it from Miss Marion's tent while she was asleep and I only hope she doesn't have to go anywhere soon, because she'll be going there in her bloomers.'

robin Hat
in a dress

'But I thought they were called Merry Men because they were always fun to be with,' said the scarecrow.

'Oh no,' said Robin Hat. 'They were only called Merry Men because they were always drunk. But enough of that. Which poor thing here needs some assistance?'

'I'm glad you asked,' replied Snow White. 'It's that strange human there. She fell from the sky and landed in a tree.'

'Oh dally wop,' said Robin Hat in his pretty dress and high heels. 'If she fell from the sky then she probably fell off a broom. In which case, I am not the one to help . . . we need a magician or two.'

'But . . .' chorused the

creatures of the forest as they tried to stop Robin Hat from getting on his mobile phone and calling Merlin's mother. But they were too late.

Bring Bring

'Hello, Merlin's mother?' said Robin Hat. 'It's Mrs Hat's son Robin here. I'm wondering if Merlin is there please?'

'He's tidying his bedroom,' said Mrs Merlin, 'and he can't possibly come to the phone.'

'But can't he just use a spell to tidy his room?' asked Robin.

'No. He has a kid's spell book and room tidying isn't in it.'

'Well perhaps you could help me then? I need to get a magic broom and zap a girl back up into the sky where she obviously came from.'

'But . . .' chorused the creatures of the forest as they tried to interrupt Robin Hat.

But they were too late.

With a *sping* and a *bang* and a *ratatat-hoho-lelala ley*, Eppie was suddenly zapped out of the forest and

found herself wide awake and riding a
broomstick.

'**Whooooooooo
aaaaaaaa!**' _{screamed}
Eppie with her mouth so wide open that
she swallowed fourteen bugs.

'Whooooooooo
oooooooooooo
oooooooaaaaa
aaaaaaaaaaaa
aaaaaaaaaaaaaa.

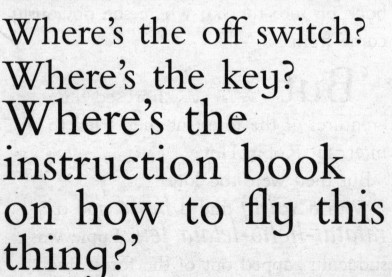

Where's the off switch?
Where's the key?
Where's the
instruction book
on how to fly this
thing?'

But of course, the only creatures who heard Eppie's question were a couple of parrots called Polly who were on their way home after a holiday on the French Riviera.

'Where's the key? Where's the instruction book!' they screeched as they imitated Eppie and laughed, 'A ha ha ha ha cackle cackle cackle.' Then the two Pollys set up a picnic on a nearby rainbow, had a cup of tea and opened some biscuits. 'Polly want a cracker?' said one parrot to the other.

'Oh no,' sobbed Eppie as she continued to whoosh and zoosh through the sky. 'What, what, what, what is going to happen to me? Here I am all alone in the sky flying as fast as a supersonic rocket with no idea where I'm going and no way of stopping myself!'

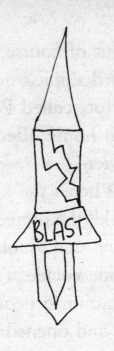

'Oh sob, sob, sob,' sobbed Eppie. 'I wonder what Zeke's doing right now.'

Strangely enough, at that moment, Zeke was just waking up . . . but then the giant did another whopper fart and knocked him unconscious again.

'Honestly,' continued Eppie, 'what is the point of putting up with a stinking, bossy boots, bully brother for years and years if the moment comes when you finally wish he were around and he is absolutely nowhere to be found! If I ever see him again, I'm going to tell him that I never want to see him again!' And with that Eppie started to shake with anger, lost her balance and nearly tipped right off the broom.

'Yaaaaaaaaaaaaaaaaaaaaaaaaaaaaaaaaaaa aaaah!' squealed Eppie as she flew upside down, hanging onto the broomstick with her legs.

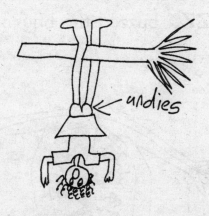

undies

'I'm sure this isn't the way you're meant to fly these things,' said Eppie as the broom's automatic seatbelts clicked into place and the driver's airbags suddenly expanded. Then, before you could say *abracadabra*, Eppie was spiralling down through the sky and heading straight for a big green pond.

'Aaaaaaaaaaaaaaaaaa aaaaaaaaaaaagh!' yelled Eppie as she flew out of control.

'Buuuuuuuuuuuuuuuuuuu uuuuuuuuuuuuzzzzzzzzzzzz zzzzzzz,' buzzed the bugs in her tummy.

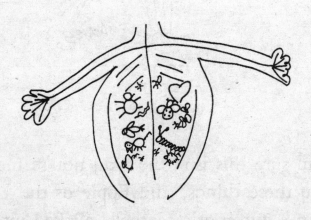

'Quaaaaaaaaaaaaaaaaaaaaa aaaaaaaaaaaaaaaaaaaaaaaaaa aaack!' quacked the ducklings as they paddled in the big green pond and watched Eppie approaching.

'Everyone duck!' laughed the parrots, but it wasn't a laughing matter, because within a millimoment Eppie had landed broom handle first, right in the middle of the pond.

'My goodness,' said Peking Duck as she cruised across the green water with her family to take a look at Eppie. 'This is without a doubt the ugliest duck I have ever seen.'

'I agree,' said Ronald Duck. 'This thing is without a doubt uglier than a baboon.'

'Well, I think she's beautiful,' said the Ugly Duckling.

'Then you're going for an eye test tomorrow afternoon because we think she looks like a toilet brush,' said Peking Duck rudely as she and Ronald Duck paddled off to Mother Goose's house for some afternoon tea and a game of golf.

'Don't worry, I'll rescue you,' quacked the Ugly Duckling as he tried to cuddle the upside-down Eppie. He shoved and he heaved and he pulled with his bill but he couldn't shift the broom from the murky mud at the bottom of the big green pond.

'Oh no,' said Eppie. 'I'm sinking! I'm sinking!'

'Have no fear,' said the Ugly Duckling. 'I will marry you and bring you a snorkel and some goggles and build you a shelter in the middle of the pond and I will—'

'Could you please hurry with the speech, Ugly Duckling,' said Eppie, 'because I'm sinking!'

'Undo your seatbelt!' called the Ugly Duckling.

'I can't,' said Eppie. 'My fingers are frozen stiff. I feel like I'm in the movie *Titanic*.'

'Would you like a piece of wood to lie on?'

'Of course I don't want a piece of wood to lie on!' bellowed Eppie. 'I want to be rescued. I want to be saved. I want a four-wheel drive or a yellow submarine to come and carry me away. I want my mother. In fact, I'm so desperate I even want my brother!'

'Well I hardly think it's the time to be choosy,' said the Ugly Duckling in a huff as he checked out his reflection in the surface of the pond. 'I mean I don't see anyone else trying to rescue you, and I hear the famous brother you go on and on about is unconscious in a giant's back pocket, completely farted out.'

a fart

'I'll rescue you,' said a big long mouth and two beady eyes as they appeared from under the water.

'But who are you?' Eppie asked.

'Why, I'm a friendly dolphin,' said the long mouth and beady eyes. 'Haven't you seen one before?'

Eppie turned her head to take a closer look and screamed the sort of piercing high-pitched scream that makes dogs on planet Pluto howl.

'Aaaaaaaaaaaaa aaaaaaaaaaaaaa aaaaaaaaaaaaaa aaaaaaaaaaaaaa aaaagh!' screamed Eppie.

'It's a crocodile!'

'So,' sulked the Ugly Duckling as he flapped and quacked and paddled away. 'I hope he eats you . . . but not until you see me turn into a beautiful swan and marry some fabulous-looking bird.'

before
(ugly duck)

after
(beautiful swan)

'All alone now, I see,' snapped the crocodile. 'What a pity there's no one here who can possibly help you.'

'My brother's coming,' Eppie lied.

'Now, I know that's not the truth,' said the crocodile.

'It is! It is the truth,' said Eppie.

'Oh really,' said the crocodile. 'Then why did I just get an e-mail from my friend the giant saying that he was emptying his pockets before doing the washing and found a little boy called Zeke?'

'Huuuuuuuuuuuuuuh!' gasped Eppie.

'Oh yes, apparently he was unconscious. So the giant put the boy to bed in one of his old smelly shoes because he wants to make sure the boy stays unconscious until the giant's birthday . . . when the boy will get eaten.'

'Huuuuuuuuuuuuuuh!' gasped Eppie.

'Oh huh indeed,' laughed the crocodile so hard that he swallowed an entire long snap-full of water and began to choke and wheeze.

'Quick,' gasped the crocodile. 'Help me, help me, I'm on the verge of drowning. Which is really and truly very embarrassing for a crocodile.'

'What will you do for me if I help you?' said Eppie.

'I promise I'll rescue you,' smirked the crocodile as he gasped for air.

'Cross your heart and hope to die?' asked Eppie.

'Oh sure,' said the crocodile. But he had his fingers crossed.

'All right,' said Eppie, 'I'll help you, but how?'

'Just stick your leg down my throat, because that will help shift any blockages.'

'Are you sure?' said Eppie.

'Of course I'm sure,' said the crocodile. 'Just hurry up and do it, because if you don't stick your leg down my throat and save me, then I won't be able to save you.'

And so very, very delicately, so as not to make her broomstick wobble and sink deeper into the muddy bottom of the pond, Eppie raised her right leg and began to place it in the crocodile's mouth.

And she would have fallen for his trick completely if it wasn't for one simple thing, and that is that the crocodile started laughing.

'Why are you laughing?' said Eppie, with her leg halfway into his mouth.

'Oh . . . umm . . . I'd like to tell you,' said the crocodile, 'but my mother taught me never to speak with my mouth full.'

'It's only half full,' said Eppie, 'so I suggest you tell me why you're laughing before I stick the broomstick in your gob as well.'

'I'm laughing because your foot tickles, of course,' said the crocodile.

'Do you want me to stop?'

'No, of course not,' said the crocodile. 'Just carry on and ignore my laughing, it's really just a nervous reaction.'

And so Eppie continued to stick her leg in the crocodile's mouth and the crocodile continued laughing. Louder and louder and louder he laughed, until all the valley echoed with his guffaws and fairytale creatures came from all over the kingdom to the edge of the pond to see what was happening.

'Oh no!' cried Rapunzel, who'd jumped out of her tower to come and see what all the kerfuffle was about. 'I suspect that's the same crocodile that ate Captain Hook's hand. In fact, I suspect that little girl is going to get her leg bitten off if we don't do something about it.'

'But what can we do?' asked the Lunchpack of Notre Dame. 'If we go in we'll get eaten too.'

'What we really need is someone who's invisible so they can rescue the girl without being seen,' said the eighth dwarf, Mopey.

'Can you see anyone here who's invisible?' asked Rapunzel.

'No,' said Rudolph the Red-eared Reindeer. 'Can you?'

'No,' said Rapunzel, 'but if someone were invisible then I wouldn't see them, and I wouldn't know they were here, and therefore I couldn't ask them to help us, could I? And so I suggest we cancel the invisible person suggestion and I shall go and rescue the girl by throwing her my long golden hair.'

'Oh how exciting!' said a wicked stepsister who had also joined the crowd. 'Do you think I could have the hair when that girl's finished with it?'

'No, I don't think so,' said Rapunzel, 'because it will still be joined to my head!'

'Oh please,' said the wicked stepsister's sister, who also happened to be wicked. 'Please can we have your hair?'

'For heaven's sake be quiet, you horrible toad heads,' said Santa, 'or you won't get anything for Christmas. Now, Rapunzel, what's the plan?'

'Well, I'm going to stand on the shore and get King Kong to throw the end of my long golden hair as close to that poor girl as he can. Are you ready, King Kong?' asked Rapunzel.

'Agub a bubb a bob,' replied King Kong.

'OK then,' said Rapunzel, 'let's get on with it.' And with that she gave the end of her hair to King Kong and described how she would like him to throw it out to the middle of the pond to help the girl with her leg stuck down a laughing crocodile's throat.

yelled Rapunzel. And King Kong threw the end of her hair so hard and so

incredibly far that Rapunzel herself was
lifted off the ground and into the air . . .
and landed smack bang next to Eppie . . .
with a leg inside the crocodile's wide
open jaws.

'A ha ha ha ha ha ha ha ha ha,'
laughed the crocodile.

'Boo hiss,' roared the
crowd.

'A ha ha ha ha ha ha ha ha ha ha ha
ha ha ha ha ha ha ha ha ha ha ha ha
ha ha ha ha ha ha ha ha ha ha ha ha
ha ha ha ha ha ha ha ha ha ha ha ha
ha ha ha ha ha ha ha ha ha ha ha ha
ha ha ha ha ha ha ha ha ha ha ha ha
ha ha ha ha ha ha ha ha ha ha ha ha
ha ha ha ha ha ha ha ha ha ha ha ha
ha ha ha ha ha ha ha ha ha ha,' laughed
the crocodile, until he was stopped by the
sudden frightening sound of a man in a
loincloth swinging through the trees yodelling,

'A ugh
a ar
a ar
arar.'

'Look, it's Tarman!' screamed all the rats who used to follow the Pied Piper but now thought Tarman was really cute.

'I love him,' screamed Pat the rat, and then promptly fainted.

'I love him too,' squeaked Cat(riona) the rat. 'I think he's absolutely gorgeous.'

'Mee tooooooooooooooo,' said little Hat(ty) the rat. 'I'd do anything for him.'

'But what about me?' said the Pied Piper. 'I thought you all said you'd follow me wherever I go.'

'That was last week,' said Nat(alie) the rat. 'Now we think Tarman's really cool.'

'But the guy wears a miniskirt!' said the

Pied Piper. 'How could that possibly be cool?'

'Well you wear tights and a two-toned hat!' said Mat(ilda) the rat.

'Oh boo buuuuuuuuuuuuuuuuuuuurr rrrrrrrrrr oh boo hoo phwatu,' said the Pied Piper as he sobbed into his flute and made a dreadful sound. 'Buuuuuuuu uuuuuuuuuuut whooooooo ooooooooooo ooo will follow meeeeeeeee eeeeeeeeeee eeeeeeeeee phughp?'

'I'll follow you, Pied Piper,' blurted the Ugly Stepmother. 'I think you're absolutely gorgeous.'

'No thanks,' said the Pied Piper. 'I've just decided to give up live show biz and the whole touring thing. I think it's time to change my career and perhaps design some handbags to match my tights.'

So off he went into the distance, with the Ugly Stepmother calling out behind him, 'Yoo hoo, darling. Wait for me. I could iron your tights for you.'

But what about Rapunzel and Eppie and the crocodile in the middle of the pond? Just what was happening to them?

Well, Eppie was tied to a broomstick that was sinking in the mud and had her leg down a crocodile's throat. While Rapunzel also had a leg stuck down the crocodile's throat and extremely messy hair.

'Don't worry, I'm coming,' warbled Tarman.

'Oh goody,' squealed the rats.

'Not to you, you stupid giggly rats,' yodelled Tarman. 'I'm coming to the lovely creatures in the pond.'

'Well thank you for being so flattering,' said the crocodile, 'and commenting on how lovely I am.'

'You're not lovely!' exclaimed Tarman. 'I was talking about the ladies who have their legs inside your gob.'

'Ooooooooooooooooh, well excuse me for living,' said the crocodile sulkily. 'Anyway, I can't talk now because I'm having guests for dinner. Might I suggest I finish eating them and then give you a call?'

'No!' screeched Tarman as he took a final leap from the very last vine, threw himself through the air . . . and landed neat and precise like a prima ballerina with one foot covering each of the crocodile's eyes.

'Help, I've gone blind,' said the crocodile as he jiggled with fear.

'Stop moving,' said Tarman, 'or I'll fall straight up your nose.'

And with that Tarman slipped up the crocodile's nose, and the crocodile sneezed and Eppie and Rapunzel were spat out of the crocodile's mouth with such gigantic force that Eppie was hurled out of the pond mud and across the pond far, far away.

Rapunzel was also hurtled through the air but due to the unfortunate fact that some of her hair was caught around the crocodile's tail (and bottom), she was forced to spend a very long time waiting for a hairdresser to come and rescue her. During that time she got to know the crocodile well and, strangely enough, the two of them got married and after the ceremony danced the night away to 'Rock Around the

Croc'. At the suggestion of Rapunzel the crocodile actually became a vegetarian, but died soon after of malnutrition. After his death Rapunzel had him stuffed and hung on the wall . . . after first removing the clock from his stomach and returning it by fairy courier to Captain Hook.

But what happened to Eppie?

Well, as I said, after being spat out of the crocodile's mouth (along with a big piece of spinach pondweed) Eppie found herself hurtling through the air, hurtling, hurtling, hurtling like a bird sitting on a rocket.

Over the pond she flew and past the bay, where Eppie glanced down and saw Pocahontas sitting on a rock singing the latest pop song by Britney.

'Oh this is scary!' screamed the flying Eppie.

'I know,' said a voice. 'That song scares me too.'

'Who are you?' asked Eppie.

'I'm the cow who jumped over the moon,' said the cow, who was on her way to jump over the moon.

Suddenly, Eppie was nearly hit by Tarman swinging past wildly and yodelling like a siren.

'Wow,' said Eppie, 'that Tarman can really swing.'

'Tarman is a bum face,' mooed the cow.

'I think he's lovely,' said Eppie.

'Lovely!' snorted the cow. 'The guy is a fruit loop. Why else would he fly through the air screaming like a monkey and dressed like a topless girl?'

'Aghag gagahah gahah agh gha gha,' warbled Tarman as he came swinging back again.

'See what I mean' said the cow haughtily. 'The guy is an absolute bum face.'

'Well, if you think Tarman's a bum face,' said Eppie as she and the cow continued to fly side by side, 'you should see my brother.'

'Is he a bum face?'

'No, he's a pig.'

'Oh, my best friend is a pig,' squealed the cow. 'Her name is Miss Piggywiggy and she's a movie star. Could you ask your brother to give her a ring?'

'OK then, if you really want me to.

What's her phone number?' said Eppie.

'No, I don't mean telephone her, I mean, give her a ring so that your pig brother can marry Miss Piggywiggy.'

'Marry Miss Piggywiggy!' squawked

Eppie. 'Don't you think they should meet each other before you arrange for them to marry? I mean, my brother really is a pig.'

'No, not at all,' said the cow who jumped over the moon. 'This is Fairytale Land where everyone always lives happily ever after. Cinderella and Prince Charming got married after just one ball and they're happy to be together. And I have two friends called the Owl and the Pussy Cat who hardly knew each other at all and they're very happy with some honey, plenty of money and a beautiful pea-green boat.'

'Well,' said Eppie, 'there's just one problem. I heard my brother is up the beanstalk and fast asleep in the giant's smelly old shoe.'

'Oh no!' said the cow. 'What will we do?'

And with that Tarman swung by one more time, yodelling away into the distance, until he landed splat against the trunk of a tree.

'See what I mean?' said the cow. 'Tarman is about as useful to you as dog poop on the bottom of your shoe.'

65

'But he was going to rescue me,' wailed Eppie.

'Don't worry,' said the cow. 'If you give me a bag of hay I'll give you a lift to the beanstalk.'

'I don't have a bag of hay!' said Eppie.

'Oh, well, do you have one million dollars?' asked the cow.

'Of course I don't,' said Eppie.

'Well, do you have one of those portable hair dryers that also curls your hair? I've always really wanted one of them,' sighed the cow.

'No,' said Eppie, 'I don't have one of them.'

'Well, bad luck,' snorted the cow as she headed for the moon. 'We can't do business then.'

'I hope you turn into hamburgers,' yelled Eppie, and then she began to sob and mumble to herself. 'I've got to get out of here.'

'Me too,' chirped a little voice.

'Me too.'

'Me too.'

'Me too.'

'Me too,' said the tiny voices of a million flying creatures rushing past.

'What's going on?' Eppie cried as she was caught in the flow of a dillion flapping wings pushing her along in their current.

But no creature or person had the time or breath to spare to explain anything to a small human.

Flap, flap, buzz, buzz. Eppie was being smothered in wings.

'Attention, all sky creatures!' said a police fairy using a daffodil as a megaphone.

'Attention, all sky creatures! There is a fire-breathing dragon in the area. We advise all flying creatures to evacuate the skies. I repeat, there is a fire-breathing dragon in the area. Please evacuate this part of the sky as quickly as you can.'

Eppie flapped her arms as fast as she could but she was slowing down instead of getting faster.

'Hurry up!' yelled the other flying creatures. 'Fly in the slow lane if you can't go fast.'

Eppie tried to manoeuvre out of the other creatures' way but all the power and boost that had thrown her out of the crocodile's mouth was now fading away.

The other creatures overtook Eppie and left her flapping feebly in the sky, trying to escape the dangerous breath of the fire-breathing dragon.

'Before long, she'll be plummeting to the ground,' wheezed the fire-breathing dragon as he watched Eppie floundering. 'I wonder if I should fry her in the sky or wait until she crashes? She'd be so much more tender after she falls,' he laughed. 'I could invite some friends over to eat her at a barbecue . . . and then I could eat my friends as well.'

Eppie flapped and wondered what to do. She could see the dragon's eyes glistening like hot coals. She could feel the gusts of hot air from his breath and she had to dodge the sparks from his flames.

'Oh this is a disaster,' said Eppie. 'I wonder if there's anything inside my pockets that could possibly save me?'

She searched in her pockets and found absolutely nothing except for an old piece of bubble gum stuck in its wrapper and a note she'd meant to give to Zeke that read, 'You are a monkey's butt.'

'Well, now I guess I'm gonna crash,' said Eppie. 'Boy, do I need something to distract me. I guess I'll eat that bubble gum, seeing as Mum's not here to bust me.' So she opened the sticky wrapper carefully as she fell from the sky and concentrated on blowing a bubble.

The bubble got bigger and bigger and bigger . . . and made the most enormous balloon . . . so Eppie floated away from the fire-breathing dragon, over the mountains (where she saw four yetis having a picnic) and over the clouds (where she spied two vampires playing ping-pong). And then she spat out her gum and landed kerplunk, diddle de doo in the middle of the forest . . . and plonk-rattle-dong deep inside the magic wishing well.

oooh pong!!!!

the damp, dark, smelly bottom of the well

'Oh dear,' said the wishing well. 'Plonk-rattle-dong! But at least you didn't bump your head like that Jack and Jill who went to fetch a pail of water and tumbled down a hill.'

'Can I make a wish to get out of here?' asked Eppie.

'Yes,' said the wishing well, 'and that's precisely my point. You see, if you didn't have to make a wish to get out of me, then you could have wished to be safe at home. But as it turns out, you have to waste your wish and there is nothing I can do about it.'

'Can't you give me another wish?' begged Eppie.

'Of course I can't. It's against magic law,' said the wishing well.

'Oh please, pretty please,' begged Eppie, trying to smile as charmingly as she could from the damp, dark, smelly bottom of the well.

'Oh all right,' said the wishing well, 'but you'll have to pay for it. Have you got a million billion trillion dillion dollars with you?'

'No, I haven't got a cent,' said Eppie.

'But even if I could only give you one dollar there'd be nothing you could buy with it.'

'That's not true,' said the wishing well, offended. 'Do you think that just because I'm a well there is nothing that I want?'

'Well, well,' said Eppie. 'It's not as though you need new clothes or a TV or a holiday in Bermuda.'

'Why not?' said the wishing well. 'I have needs too. I would love to own a sports car or go skiing in Europe, and that is precisely what I will do when you give me a million billion trillion dillion dollars.'

'But I haven't got a million billion trillion dillion dollars,' said Eppie, 'though I really wish I did!'

And all of a sudden Eppie was surrounded by millions and dillions of thousand-dollar bills.

'Ah, thank you,' said the well, 'I'll take

that as payment. And now for your final wish. I suppose you wish you were out of the well.'

'Final wish! You're kidding!' said Eppie. 'Wishing for the money wasn't a real wish.'

'I'm sorry, but you did say I wish.'

'You mean that even after I give you all this money I still only have one wish?'

'Yurp,' burped the well.

'I just can't believe this!' said Eppie. 'You are even more selfish than my Aunt Flowerhead, who only gives us IOUs for Christmas. I wish you weren't a magic wishing well at all and were just a simple little hole in the ground!'

And with a bing and a bong and a phwat-bam-boo the magic wishing well disappeared and Eppie found herself standing up to her ankles in a little hole that was overflowing with millions and dillions of thousand-dollar notes.

'Oh, how delightful!' said the emperor in his new clothes, who was walking by at that moment wearing absolutely nothing but his boxers. 'Just imagine how many more wonderful clothes I could buy if all those dollars were mine.'

'Oh yes,' said all the dukes and duchesses and maids and manservants who were following the emperor and were too chicken to tell him he was nearly in the nuddy, 'imagine how many beautiful clothes you could buy if all those dollars were yours . . .'

'Well they're not yours,' laughed a wicked voice. 'They're soon to be mine, mine, mine!'

And Eppie looked up and saw that hovering above was a wicked witch on her broom.

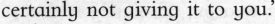

'The money is mine,' Eppie said to the witch, 'and I'm certainly not giving it to you.'

'We'll see about that!' laughed the wicked witch, and she turned the emperor into a weed (wearing underpants) and turned all his followers into bindi-eyes and then disappeared on her magic broomstick.

Eppie stood in the hole surrounded by thousand-dollar notes and quietly began to sob. Deer and rabbits came from the forest to stand in a circle around her. They watched the tears flow from her eyes and wondered what to do.

'Don't be sad,' said Mambi. 'It will be all right. You can come and live with us.' But just as Mambi approached Eppie to lick away her tears Eppie burst out laughing.

'Something's tickling my feet,' she giggled hysterically. Something's tickling both of my feet.

Stop, stop, stop, stop!' But the tickling continued . . . and Eppie began to rise from the hole. In fact she was lifted right out of the ground . . . and found herself high above everyone else, standing on Malice in Wonderland's head.

'Boy, have I got a headache,' said Malice to the rabbits, unaware of where Eppie was. 'I'm glad to be back where things are what they seem, because it's taken me ages to dig out from under the ground.'

'I'm sorry,' said Eppie as she jumped off Malice's head.

'Who are you?' asked Malice.

'I'm Eppie,' said Eppie.

'You look as though you're in a bit of bother – would you like me to help you?' asked Malice sweetly.

'Oh, yes please,' replied Eppie gratefully. 'I'm so glad I've found a girl just like me who I know I can trust.'

'Well, first,' said Malice, with her long golden hair shining in the sunlight and her twinkling blue eyes matching the blue collar and blue bow of her pretty dress, 'first we must gather all this money and put it in my purse.'

So that's exactly what everyone did. But Eppie and the animals were taking their time, singing and dancing as they worked.

'Hurry up, hurry up!' said Malice angrily. 'We're running out of time. The spell only lasts for thirty minutes.'

'What?' said the fly on Peter Rabbit's nose.

'What spell are you talking about?' asked Mambi.

'Oh um,' mumbled Malice, 'the um, er, um, ah . . . the money spell of course. Now do as I say,' whispered Malice to Mambi, 'or I'll turn you into a floor rug!'

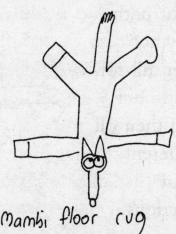

the Mambi floor rug

It took them nearly twenty-nine minutes, but sure enough, Eppie and the animals managed to pick up every single thousand-dollar note and put it safely inside Malice's purse.

'Ha ha ha ha ha ha ha!' screeched Malice. 'Just in time. Thank you for giving me all this money before I turn back into a WITCH!' And with that a black pointy hat began to grow on her head and a wart appeared on the end of her nose.

'Oh no!' said Eppie and Mambi and Peter Rabbit. 'Quick, run down that path.'

And that's what they did. They all ran down paths . . . but unfortunately they all ran down different paths going in different directions.

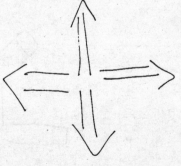

Pretty soon Eppie realized that she was all alone. So she stopped, sat down on a toadstool and wondered what to do. An angel appeared and played the harp to her, while a Worcestershire cat pounced from a tree and danced a little jig until Eppie, who was very tired and hungry, sobbed and fell asleep.

While she was asleep Eppie was visited by a beautiful fairy godmother, who told her to find her brother and rescue him.

'Why?' said Eppie as she snored. 'It's so much quieter here without him.'

'Because Zeke is your brother and you must look after each other,' said the fairy godmother. 'And if you don't help him and get him safely home your mother will never ever let you watch anything on TV except for the news and the cricket!'

And with that Eppie woke with a start, determined to find Zeke, because if there's anything worse than not watching telly it's being forced to watch the cricket! But where was she to go, how was she to get to the beanstalk, and who was she to ask for directions and help?

The Worcestershire cat just grinned at Eppie and offered no help at all, and the angel had left several minutes ago, to play the harp at the giant's birthday ball.

'Hi!' tweeted a bird as he crash-landed right by Eppie's feet. 'I'm Chirpie. Air, Land and Sea Rescue have sent word that you're in need of some assistance. They tried to get the Road Sprinter to help you, but he's been run over, which just goes to show, you really shouldn't run on the roads. Now, follow me because I know a path of breadcrumbs that we can follow to a happy ending.'

And so they wandered through the forest, past Aladdin's cave and Little Red Riding Hood's house and the cottage where the three bears live.

'Can't we stop here and ask for directions?' asked Eppie.

'Of course not,' said Chirpie. 'All the usual residents have gone away to rest and relax at one of those health farms.

Even characters from books need a break sometimes from the pressures of being so nice, you know. So, we must just follow the crumbs until we get to the Mellow Brick Road and then we'll find the Wizard of Was, ask for directions to the beanstalk and get your brother back safely again.'

'Do you think someone could put a spell on him to make sure he's nice to me for ever?' asked Eppie.

'This is only Fairytale Land,' said Chirpie, stopping to pat Eppie on the shoulder with his canary-yellow wing. 'I'm afraid there isn't enough magic in the whole wide place to make a brother be nice to his sister.'

Suddenly, there was a loud miaow followed by a pounce, and Chirpie was swallowed by the Worcestershire cat in one simple great big gulp.

'Oh no,' groaned Eppie. 'Now Chirpie's dead!'

'No I'm not,' said a muffled voice that seemed to be coming from the cat's bottom. 'The Worcestershire cat swallowed me whole, so I'm actually only trapped in here.'

'Do you want me to help you?' said Eppie to the cat's bottom.

'No,' said Chirpie from inside the Worcestershire cat. 'I'll wait until the cat falls asleep and then wriggle my way out of here. In the meantime, I'll just try to relax and perhaps whistle some tunes.'

'Goodbye, Chirpie,' said Eppie to the cat's bottom.

'Goodbye, Eppie,' said the cat's bottom . . . umm, I mean Chirpie.

cat's bottom

85

Eppie continued to follow the bread-crumb path until she came to a most wonderful house in the woods, which was absolutely covered in lollies.

'Oh good,' said Eppie to herself. 'I can eat here and not have to worry at all about being so hungry at the giant's feast that I accidentally eat one of Zeke's fingers.'

And Eppie began to eat the wonderful candy house. She started in the lollipop garden, of course, and then ate the caramel button doorknob. Then she ate the marshmallow chairs on the front veranda and the fairy-bread shutters on the windows. She ate and ate and ate and ate and ate and ate and ate and ate all those wonderful lollies until, suddenly, her brain sent out an alarm.

'Warning! Warning! Sugar overload!'

And Eppie started to giggle and sing very loudly and run round and round the house.

'Yipppeeeeee!'

she shouted as she ran faster than a triped snake with fleas in his ears.

'Yipppeee, yippeee eeeeeee, yipppeeeee eeeeeeeeeeeeeeeeeeeeee eeeeeeeeeeeeeeeeeeeeee eeeeeeeeeeeeeeeeeeeeee eeeeeeeeeee.'

'Oh for heaven's sake!' said the old lady who normally lived in a shoe but was renting the witch's candy house for the holidays. 'No wonder the witch eats these children, they really are very annoying.'

Quietly she rose from the rocking chair, turned on the oven and began to set the table. 'The little girl will be getting thirsty soon, so I'll cook her when she comes to the door for a drink.'

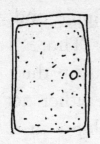 Sure enough, only a few minutes later Eppie knocked on the door. 'Hello, dear,' said the old lady who normally lived in a shoe.

'Hello,' said Eppie. 'I was wondering if you might have a glass of water I could drink?'

'No, I don't have any water,' said the old lady. 'But I do have some lovely red sugary cordial. Why don't you take a seat by the fire and I'll get a glass of it for you.'

'I'm very sorry,' said Eppie, 'but I can't sit down. I need to keep running round and round.'

'Well then,' said the old lady, who was desperate for Eppie to have so much sugar that she collapsed from being over-energized, 'I'll give you a drink bottle full of green lemonade and a straw so you can drink it as you run.'

Then she gave the bottle to Eppie and had a little chuckle to herself. 'That sugar hit will more than likely tip the little girl over the edge. She'll either get completely exhausted and collapse in a heap or else all the sugar will bubble in her brain and she'll have a fuse function overload.' And sure enough, both things happened at once ... and Eppie collapsed by the chocolate biscuit door in a little girl heap.

'Good,' said the old lady who normally lived in a shoe as she lifted Eppie into a wheelbarrow and pushed her through the back door and into the kitchen. 'This little girl will be so much easier to cook without all that wriggling around. But first I'd better check the fridge and see what vegetables I can prepare.'

And so the old woman who normally lived in a shoe went to the fridge to look for her favourite vegetables, which were

Brussels sprouts, pumpkin and courgettes. But to her horror not a one was there.

'Oh no,' she said. 'I can't have a meal without vegetables, that's far too unhealthy for me. I'll have to go to the neighbours' and see if they have a couple of veggies or three.'

So she wheeled Eppie to Old Mother Hubbard's house and explained to her that she was about to eat the little girl but unfortunately didn't have any vegetables.

'Neither do I,' said Old Mother Hubbard. 'Why don't you try the old woman who swallowed a fly?'

So the old woman who normally lived in a shoe pushed the wheelbarrow along over the hill to ask the old woman who swallowed a fly . . . but she didn't have any vegetables either.

'Perhaps you could try asking at the house where the third little pig lives,' said the old lady who swallowed a fly. 'I understand she has some fresh vegetables that she's keeping until they go completely off and can be turned into a disgusting swill.'

'OK,' said the old lady who normally lived in a shoe, 'I'll go and try over there.' And so she pushed Eppie in the wheelbarrow all the way up the hill, past a crumbled pile of straw, past a crumbled pile of sticks, and up to a house made completely of brick. And she knocked on the door.

'Hello, Poopsy,' said Miss Piggywiggy as she answered the door. 'My goodness, what have we here!'

'It's a child I'm going to eat,' said the old woman who normally lived in a shoe, 'and I was wondering if you had any vegetables that I could balance out my meal with.'

'I see,' said Miss Piggywiggy, eyeing the wheelbarrow and the sleeping girl inside it. 'Tell me, where did you happen to get this human?'

'She came into my garden,' replied the old lady who normally lived in a shoe.

'Well,' said Miss Piggywiggy, becoming more and more certain that lying inside this wheelbarrow was her future sister-in-law, 'I will give you as many vegetables as you like. In fact I'll give you a whole wheelbarrow full. Let's take the child out of the barrow and I'll fill it up for you.' And off Miss Piggywiggy went to the vegetable garden and returned with an entire wheelbarrow full of Brussels sprouts, courgettes and pumpkins.

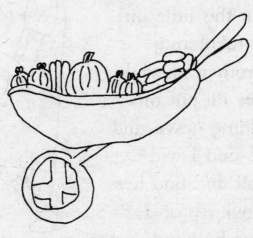

'There,' said Miss Piggywiggy, 'now why don't you take this load home and then come back for the child.'

'Okey-dokey,' said the old lady who normally lived in a shoe, 'that is in fact an excellent idea. I'll set off right away.' And she did.

'Oh fabulous,' said Miss Piggywiggy in a loud and excited voice once the old lady who normally lived in a shoe had run off.
'The cow who jumped over the moon told me all about this little girl and her fabulously piggy brother, so while she sleeps I'll put on my wedding gown and then she and I will toddle off and find her brother, who is also my future husband.'

Eppie slept while Miss Piggywiggy unpacked the long white wedding dress she had bought at the garage sale of Beauty and the Beast. Then Miss Piggywiggy squeezed herself like a sausage into the dress and telephoned Dorothy in Kansas to see if she could please borrow the red shoes she'd left under the house the last time her house crashed nearby. And then, all dressed and beautiful, Miss Piggywiggy borrowed Thumbelina's big toy pram, placed Eppie inside and began pushing Eppie all the way to the little farm where she knew Jack's mother lived. But before Miss Piggywiggy even got to the corner of the street she bumped into Pin-okey-dokey-o.

'Where are you going in your wedding dress, Miss Piggywiggy?' asked Pin-okey-dokey-o.

'I'm going off to get married,' replied Miss Piggywiggy loudly.

'Oh my, well ain't he the lucky fella!' said Pin-okey-dokey-o as his nose began to grow. 'You wouldn't be marrying a groom who's up the beanstalk with the giant, would you?'

'Why yes, I am,' blushed Miss Piggywiggy. 'But tell me, why do you ask?'

'Well, it's just that the incey wincey spider told me that the giant is currently preparing a feast and is about to eat the fella.'

'Are you telling the truth?' demanded Miss Piggywiggy.

'Is my nose shrinking?' said Pin-okey-dokey-o.

'Why yes,' said Miss Piggywiggy, 'it would appear that it is. In which case I'd better run along.' And Miss Piggywiggy went on her way.

'By the way, Miss Piggywiggy, you look absolutely lovely,' yelled Pin-okey-dokey-o as Miss Piggywiggy tottered away and Pin-okey-dokey-o's  nose began to grow once again.

Of course, it wasn't hard to tell which was Jack's mother's house because she had an enormous beanstalk in her garden. The problem was, however, that Jack's mother wasn't at home and the entrance to the giant's beanstalk was not only locked but guarded by one billion barking bulldogs who had been trained by Frankfurtstein.

'OK, well there goes that idea,' said Miss Piggywiggy as she eyed the gate to the beanstalk. 'We have a time problem and a height problem, but other than that everything is under control. Pin-okey-dokey-o seems a wise and helpful chap –

I think we'll go back and ask him what to do.'

When Miss Piggywiggy found Pin-okey-dokey-o, he was trying hard to find someone to tell the truth to so that his nose would shrink. But as soon as he said, 'My dear Miss Piggywiggy, how nice to see you once more,' his nose began to grow.

'Hello again,' said Miss Piggywiggy. 'I'm sorry to interrupt, but I was wondering if you could possibly think of a way to get up to the giant's castle without actually using the beanstalk.'

'Well, you could always try the magic bed that the genie sits on at the end of

the lane. Come with
me and I'll show
you where he is. I'm
sure he'll be more
than delighted to
help you out today,'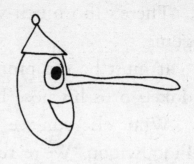
said Pin-okey-dokey-o as his nose grew
once again.

'All right,' said the genie. 'You can
borrow my magic bed but you have to
pay for the petrol.'

'Well, if you can wait,' said Miss
Piggywiggy, 'we will bring some of the
giant's treasure and that will more than
pay for the petrol.'

'All right,' said the genie, 'that sounds
good to me. On you get and off you go,
but try to be back by tea.'

It was all well and good to say 'on you
get and off you go', but right at that
particular point it seemed the magic bed
wasn't going anywhere.

'There's too much weight on it,' said the genie.

'It must be the pram,' said Pin-okey-dokey-o as his nose began to grow again.

'What else can we do?' snorted Miss Piggywiggy. 'We're running out of time!'

'I know, I'll call my mate Peter Saucepan. He'll be able to fly you up and maybe even back again,' said Pin-okey-dokey-o as his nose stretched like plas-ticine.

Pin-okey-dokey-o put his wooden fingers to his mouth and made the most deafening whistling sound. Then, within seconds, a really cool, cute guy appeared and of course Eppie woke up.

'Oh my goodness,' Eppie murmured as she looked at Peter Saucepan. 'I think I've fallen in love.'

'Hello, beautiful,' said Peter Saucepan to Eppie. 'Do you feel like going flying?'

'Sure,' said Eppie.

'Well then, hop on my back,' said Peter Saucepan with a smile.

'Now wait a minute!' bellowed Miss Piggywiggy. 'Don't forget I'm coming too!'

And so Eppie and Miss Piggywiggy climbed on Peter Saucepan's back and . . . he collapsed in a heap on the ground.

'Get me a doctor,' groaned Peter Saucepan.

'I already have,' said Pin-okey-dokey-o

as his nose took such a big long stretch
that he could no longer see the end of it.

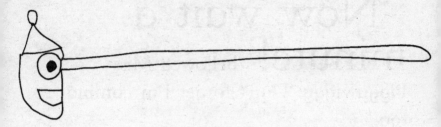

'It looks like we have no choice but to
walk along Pin-okey-dokey-o's nose as
though it were a bridge to the top of the
beanstalk,' said Miss Piggwiggy.

'But what about Peter Saucepan?' asked
Eppie, broken-hearted.

'Don't worry,' said Pin-okey-dokey-o.
'He'll still be here when you get back
down.' And then Pin-okey-dokey-o's nose
took an almighty stretch to the sky and
Miss Piggywiggy and Eppie climbed on.

On and on and on they walked, huffing
and puffing as they made the steep climb
until they began to smell the aroma of a
feast cooking.

'Run!' said Miss Piggywiggy as she trotted along. 'Run! They're about to eat my darling.'

'It's a bit hard to run uphill,' said Eppie.

'Well bad luck, pencil legs,' said Miss Piggywiggy. 'Run fast anyway!' And run they did, on and on and on until they came to the gates of the giant's castle and Miss Piggywiggy said, 'Quick, hop on my back!' and they barged straight through the wall.

Now they were galloping up the driveway, through the castle and out to the lawns, and there they saw the crowd, who were all watching the  giant as he picked up the most enormous skewer and got ready to barbecue the still dozing Zeke.

'Stop!' yelled Miss Piggywiggy as she ground to such a sudden halt that Eppie flew right over her head and landed in the giant's birthday cake.

eppie's legs

HAPPY BIRTHDAY

'Stop! I beg you to stop!'

yelled Miss Piggywiggy.

'Why, Piggywiggy,' said the giant, who everyone knew was secretly in love with Miss Piggywiggy. 'You are perfectly in time for the frying of the entrée.'

'Oh my dear giant, I beg of you, if you love me at all, please don't cook that food. I am on a diet just for you and would much prefer to eat the whole thing raw.'

'The whole thing, Miss Piggywiggy?' queried the giant.

'Of course,' replied Miss Piggywiggy.

So the giant brought sleepy Zeke to Miss Piggywiggy on a plate with some parsley on his forehead.

'Aaaaaaaaa

aaaaaaaaaaaaaaag hhhhhhh!' squealed Miss

Piggywiggy when she took one look at Zeke. 'This boy is not a pig!'

'Well no, he's not exactly a pig, but don't you agree that he is revolting?' said Eppie quietly.

'I have been tricked!' roared Miss

Piggywiggy. 'Take the boy and girl away and cook them both while I marry the giant instead.'

'Yipppppeee eeeeeeeeeeee eeeee!' whooped the giant.

The Elton John CD started to play and

the giant was so happy that he started to dance. And he danced so enthusiastically that with all his shaking and bouncing about, anything lighter than a deep-sea monster who'd been eating bricks was boinged right off the castle grounds and fell over the edge. So witches and goblins, elves and warlocks tumbled to the land way below . . . and so did Zeke and Eppie.

'Where are you, Zeke?' screamed Eppie as she clung to the edge of a cloud. 'I can't hold on much longer, Zeke. Please come and get me!' And then she fell.

Down.

Down.

Down.

Until all of a sudden, a smelly but not so sleepy brother appeared riding on the goose that laid the golden egg, who had a part-time job as a taxi.

'Where would you like to go?' asked the goose after Eppie had landed neatly on her back.

'Um,' said Zeke, 'we want to go home. Do you know where there's a bus stop so we can catch a bus that will take us out of Fairytale Land?'

'No I don't,' said the goose that laid the golden egg. 'The only stops of any sort that we have here are full stops. Do you think they might do?'

'Yes,' said Eppie, 'we'll give that a try.' And so that's where Zeke and Eppie climbed off the goose that laid the golden egg and paid with the only things they could spare . . . Zeke's Barbie doll undies.

'Oh look!' said the goose delightedly after Zeke had snuck behind a tree and the goose had tried the undies on. 'They're perfect!'

When they got to the full stop, Zeke and Eppie found a door with a simple sign that said Exit.

'Well, if all goes well,' said Zeke, 'we'll walk through this door, get out of the book and be back in our world. We'll find ourselves in Mum's lap and then we'll only have to be stretched to our regular size and life will be back to normal again.'

'Good luck to us,' said Eppie.

'Yes, good luck to us,' said Zeke. Then they shook hands, wiped each other's germs off on their shirts, opened the exit

door and went through.

It was very dark. Very, very dark. And there were no lights or maps to follow. Eppie and Zeke stumbled and tripped and crawled their way along the tunnel.

'Do we turn right here?' asked Eppie.

'No, we should turn left,' said Zeke.

'You don't know any more than me, Zeke. I think we should turn right,' bossed Eppie.

'No, we'll go left,' said Zeke angrily.

'Well, Zeke, if we can't agree then we'll have to compromise and just go straight ahead,' said Eppie. And that's what they did until they came to a ladder, which they climbed up until they landed thump in the pitch dark once more.

'Do you know where we are?' said Zeke.

'No,' said Eppie. 'Do you?'

'Nooooooooooooooooooooooooooooo,' said Zeke. 'I think we may be in our world, but I really can't see a thing.'

Suddenly they heard the whistle of a small train that pulled up right in front of them. So Zeke and Eppie climbed aboard, took a seat and waited for the conductor.

'Where are you going?' asked the conductor as he came by selling tickets.

'We don't know,' said Eppie. 'Where can we go?'

'Well, you've missed Dream World, Real World and Fantasy World, so I'm afraid the only stop left is your mother's Nightmare World.'

'What do you mean? What are you talking about?' yelled Zeke.

'Why, this is your mother's train of thought,' said the conductor, 'and she's having a nightmare about you two right now.'

With a terrible lurch the train came to a grinding halt and Eppie and Zeke flew out of the window and landed on a pirate ship.

'Why, hello there,' said the captain, who also happened to be an estate agent. 'Welcome to your mother's nightmare . . .'

TO BE CONTINUED

About the illustrators:

Zeke

Zeke was born in 1988 and is a fun-loving, phone-hogging Sagittarian. He likes surfing, cricket, football, chocolate drinks and teasing his little sister. When he grows up he wants to be incredibly rich so that he can live in a mansion and hire slaves to do all the work his mum does for him now.

Eppie

Eppie was born in 1991 and looked like a very pretty worm. She loves dancing, singing, composing songs and screaming loudly whenever her brother comes near. When she grows up she wants to be a banker, singer, actor, writer and teacher. And she also wants to marry a prince.

GRETEL KILLEEN

My Sister's a
Yo-yo

When Eppie falls into a pothole, gets **squashed** to the size of a **strawberry** and becomes completely **entangled** in her brother Zeke's **yo-yo**, Zeke only has a day to get her back to normal. What follows is a **hilarious** high tale of **escape**, theft, bullies, **brats**, goody-goodies, garbage trucks, **magic** lamps, **scabs**, snot, bribery, **bravery**, a blind mum, a fat nurse, a **skinny teacher** and a boy on a bicycle covered in something **very unsavoury** – and that's only the beginning!

'Short-every-second inventive fun'
JACQUELINE WILSON

0099433680

£3.99

GRETEL KILLEEN

When Eppie gets **squished** to the size of a strawberry, ends up **flying** round the world, landing on planet sock and about to be kidnapped by a **handsome alien** prince, it's up to her brother Zeke to rescue her. What follows is a **laugh-a-minute** adventure full of short-sighted cats, space rockets, **burps**, possums, owls, **goodies**, **baddies**, galactic battles, **movie stars**, superstars, false **moustaches**, girls' nighties, flying horses, footballs, diamonds, **lovesick Martians** and motorbike rides with the man in the moon – and that's all before mum wakes up.

'Madly inventive and very funny'
JACQUELINE WILSON

0099433672

£3.99

GRETEL KILLEEN

My Sister's a
Sea Slug

When Eppie and Zeke get
stretched like spaghetti it's
only a matter of time before
they are **sucked** down the
plughole and into a new
adventure. What follows
is a **giggle-filled** non-stop
underwater **romp**, with man-eating
seaweed, pirates in petticoats, secret
castles, **magic mermaids**, fat fisherman,
splendid speedy sea cycles, **elastic**
eels, and **supersonic** horses
. . . and that's all before breakfast!

0099448076

£3.99

GRETEL KILLEEN

My Sister's a
Burp

When the teeny-weeny Zeke and Eppie are accidentally **swallowed** by their mum they **need** to find a way to **safety** but first they need to **wake up** Mum's brain. What follows is a **chock-a-block adventure** full of **jealous germs, evil eyes, bouncing bottoms, hysterical hair, ticklish teeth, arm armies** and **tap-dancing toes** . . . and that's all before Mum realises that Zeke and Eppie are **even missing.**

'Snort-every-second inventive fun'
JACQUELINE WILSON

0099448084